Pin, The Reluctant Knight

PIN,
The Reluctant Knight

Written and Illustrated
by William Wiesner

W · W · NORTON & COMPANY · INC ·

NEW YORK

jW 6374pi

To my friend
Hans Fybel

Once upon a time there was a tailor named Pin. Though he was still very young, he was extremely skillful—quite an artist in his profession. But he lived in a little house far from any city, and his customers were simple farmers who came only to have their old clothes patched. Often Pin yearned for an order that would be equal to his skill and show what an excellent tailor he really was.

One day a coach drawn by four magnificent horses stopped in front of the tailor's house, and out of it stepped the Lord Chamberlain himself!

"Master Pin," said he, "I need an elegant out-fit for the great ball that will take place at the court in five days. The court tailor is so busy he cannot accept another order. I hear you are a quick and skillful tailor. Here is the material. Take my measurements right now."

Pin was delighted, for the day that would give him a chance to show his art to the world had finally arrived! Happily, he took careful measure-ments for the silk suit and velvet cap. Then the grand gentleman stepped back into his coach and rode away.

Pin set to work immediately. Squatting on his tailor's bench, he cut the material and started to sew with such speed that the needle seemed to fly through the air. Day and night he worked on the magnificent outfit, and, finally, three days later, the gorgeous suit and the velvet cap were finished and ready to be delivered.

By that time Pin was so exhausted he could hardly keep his eyes open. Quickly he undressed, slipped under his blanket, blew out the candle, and fell asleep. He was so terribly tired he forgot to cover the coal-pan that he used to heat the iron. Later, a spark dropped on the wooden floor. It began to burn immediately, and soon the entire house was in flames.

The heat and the smoke woke Pin from his deep sleep. He jumped from his bed, slipped into his shoes, grabbed the suit and cap, a pair of scissors, a needle and thread, and was out of the house in one leap!

There he stood in his nightshirt, hugging the precious suit, sadly watching his house burn down to a heap of charred timber. He was glad that at least he had saved the suit; and he was certain that once he was paid for it, he would have enough money to build a new little shop. To make sure his beautiful work would arrive unharmed at the Lord Chamberlain's palace, he decided to deliver it himself.

The night was cold, and Pin shivered in the piercing wind. Quickly he put on the Lord Chamberlain's clothes, saying to himself, "Tomorrow morning I'll be sure to find a charitable soul who will lend me some pants and a coat so that I can take off this expensive garment and deliver it properly."

He started out immediately, for the Lord Chamberlain's castle was many miles away. But the night was very dark, and in his excitement Pin soon missed the right road and took a path that led through a dark wood. When he saw that he was lost, Pin tried another path, hoping it would lead to the highway. But the dark wood seemed to be under some evil spell, and the path kept getting narrower and narrower, steeper and steeper. It finally led him into a dark ravine. Poor Pin felt utterly lost, but there was nothing to do but stumble on and on. After some time he came upon a rocky cliff on one side of the ravine; soon he noticed a thin ray of light coming through a crevice in the rock.

With renewed hope, Pin thought, "Perhaps here I shall find a warm place to sleep." He squeezed through the narrow opening and found himself in a cave. In the middle was a fire, and five evil-looking fellows sat around it.

"Hey, look what a fine visitor we have," shouted the leader of the gang. "Out with your purse!"

Pin was struck dumb with fright. The robbers searched him from head to foot to find his money, but all they discovered was the little bag with scissors, needle, and thread. They were furious at not finding anything more valuable.

"Hey, boss," they shouted, brandishing their daggers, "let's get rid of him, right here and now!"

"Come now, use your heads," said the leader. "With these clothes he must be a rich nobleman. We can get a high ransom for such a fine lord."

They all agreed and gave Pin food and drink and a place to sleep near the fire. Such a valuable prisoner must be treated well. Then they all lay down in front of the narrow exit and were soon asleep.

Pin cursed the rich garments that had gotten him into such trouble. He was terrified to imagine what might happen when the robbers found out he was nothing but a poor tailor. He searched frantically for a way to escape. But there was none. The sleeping robbers blocked the exit, and any attempt to get out would awaken them.

Suddenly he had an idea. He took out his needle and thread and very cautiously sewed the robbers' sleeves together until they were attached to each other like a string of sausages. Then he climbed over them and ran away as fast as his legs would carry him.

He could hear the angry shouts of the robbers as they tried to chase him, but they were stuck in the narrow crevice, tightly sewn to each other and unable to move backward or forward.

Pin ran on and on until he reached the end of the ravine. There he dropped down, utterly exhausted, and looked around. A wide, peaceful valley stretched before him. In the distance he saw a walled town with a beautiful castle in the midst of it.

"There I shall certainly be able to get rid of these bothersome clothes, so that I won't always be taken for a nobleman," thought Pin, and he started hopefully toward the town. But as he walked ahead, he grew very uneasy, for the whole valley seemed very strange. There was not a soul on the highway; no cattle grazed in the meadows; no wheat or corn grew in the fields.

When Pin entered the town the few people he met tottered along sadly. Their cheeks were hollow and their eyes looked sorrowful.

More and more curious, he walked on until he reached the castle, where he saw a proclamation posted on the gate. Pin stopped and started to read. The proclamation said:

To all Noblemen, Knights, and Brave Men of Rank! An evil giant ravages our land and eats us out of house and home. My bravest knights have been unable to defeat him. Now our fields lie barren, our larders arc empty, and we are on the brink of starvation. The giant will not leave until he gets the princess for his wife.

Noblemen, Knights, Men of Rank! Whoever of you defeats the giant shall marry the princess and be heir to my throne!

Your Majesty the King

While Pin the tailor was reading the proclamation, the people who passed stopped and stared at him, attracted by his magnificent garb. Soon he was surrounded by a curious crowd. He could hear people saying, "At last a knight has come again to help us," or "What a strong and handsome nobleman! I am sure he will defeat the giant."

The tailor became greatly alarmed and tried in vain to be heard. "Come," shouted the people, "we'll take you to the king!" There was no way out, for the excited crowd would not let him go.

"Now I am in a pretty pickle," thought Pin.

But by this time he was already in the throne room, standing before the king and the princess.

"Welcome! Welcome!" said the king. "Are you willing to fight the giant?"

A great hush fell over the entire room. Every man held his breath. Pin's hair stood on end at the mere thought of such a fight. Then he looked at the princess and thought of the terrible fate that would befall her if she fell into the hands

of the giant. So he gathered up his courage and spoke in a firm voice. "I shall fight the giant, Your Majesty."

"Hurrah," shouted all the people, so loudly that the walls shook.

"Bravely spoken," said the king. He stepped down from the throne and clapped Pin on the back. "In my armory you may choose the best armor and the sharpest sword."

"Oh no," answered Pin the tailor, "I have no use for sword and armor. Have five bales of green cloth and five bales of red cloth carried up to the giant's cave. That is all I shall need."

Everybody was amazed at this peculiar request; but they did as he wished.

The giant's cave was high up on a steep mountain, and only with great effort and exertion were the heavy bales dragged up to it. Now all the people went away, and Pin stood alone in front of the entrance to the cave.

He drew a deep breath and shouted, "Come out, Mister Giant, come out! I am the most famous tailor in the world and have come to offer you my services."

The loud calls woke the giant from his sleep. Furious, he crawled out from his cave and drew himself up to his full height. When Pin saw the monster his heart sank into his boots, for the giant was twenty feet tall, and his hands were bigger than a door.

"The deuce! How dare you wake me up," roared the giant. "I'll give it to you, you whipper-snapper. Knights like you I catch like flies."

Lifting his cudgel the giant went at him. But Pin the tailor was a nimble fellow and, light as a feather, he leaped to and fro, left and right, while the giant stamped clumsily around him.

When he tried to strike Pin with his cudgel, he hit only the ground with a loud bang, for Pin had already jumped away.

After a while the giant grew tired of this useless stomping around. He sat down and growled, "You may look like a knight, but you aren't one. You have no armor and no sword. Instead of fighting you hop around like a flea. Come now, who are you really?"

With a courteous bow, Pin answered, "As I told you before, I am the most famous tailor in the world. I heard that you are going to marry the princess and have come to take your measurement for your wedding suit."

"Nonsense," said the giant rudely. "I need no such frippery, for I am a handsome, well-built giant."

"That is somewhat exaggerated," said Pin. "You are the DIRTIEST, RAGGEDEST, and UGLIEST giant I have ever seen. But I can turn you into an elegant, fine-looking giant in no time at all."

At that Pin started to unroll the red and green bales of cloth, continuing, "If you want to find favor in the eyes of the princess, you must wear red trousers with a green coat. That is the latest fashion."

Somewhat startled the giant asked, "Could you really turn me into a gentleman?"

"Of course! I shall turn you into a gentleman; you can be sure of it," answered Pin.

Taking one bale of red cloth after the other he wound the cloth round both the giant's legs so that the giant couldn't move them. Then he took needle and thread and sewed the cloth firmly together.

"Ugh," groaned the giant, "the trousers are too tight."

"Tight, but smart," answered the tailor.

Then he took the green cloth, saying, "Now I am going to make the coat."

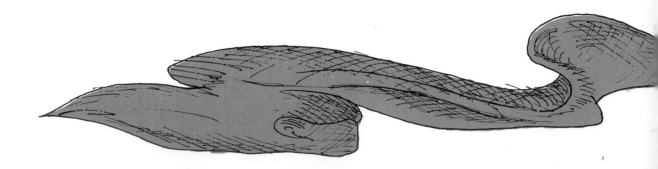

Pin wound the cloth around the giant's upper body so that the giant's arms were inside and he couldn't move at all. Again Pin sewed the cloth together with firm stitches. Now the giant was swaddled from top to bottom like a giant baby.

"Ugh," groaned the giant, "the coat is much too tight."

"Tight, but smart," said Pin, and he gave the wrapped-up giant a push so that he rolled down the steep mountain.

And he rolled on and on until he disappeared forever and was never seen again.

"Good riddance," said Pin with a sigh of relief. "But now it's high time that I got rid of these bothersome clothes." Once again he started out to find the Lord Chamberlain's palace.

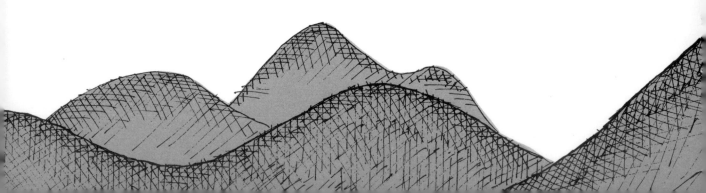

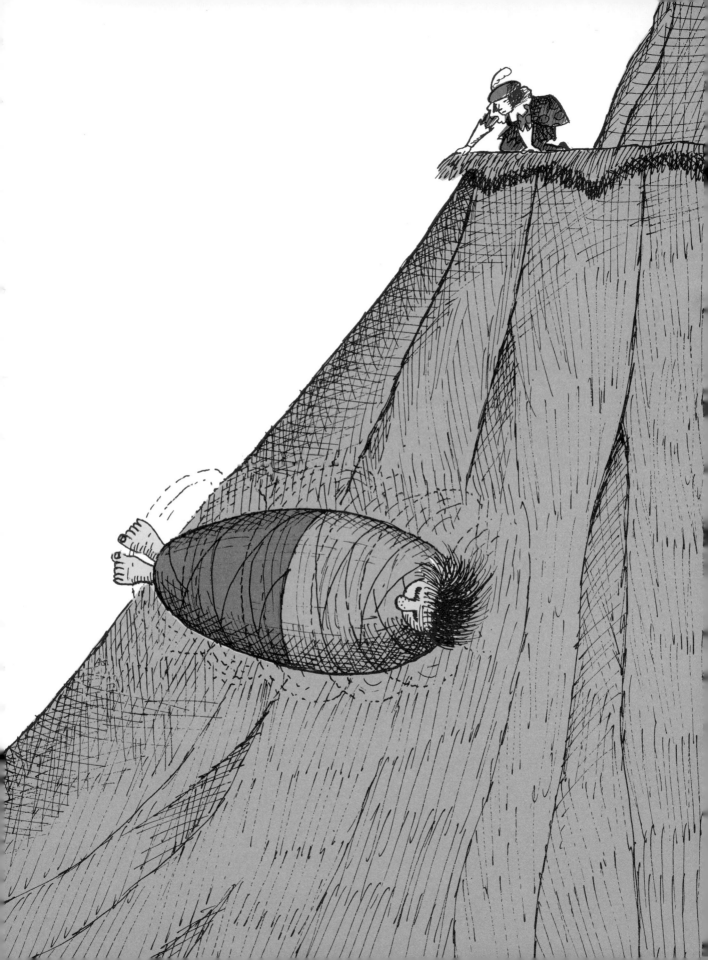

He had taken only a few steps, however, when a shout went up from all sides, "Hurrah, hurrah, long live our liberator!" From all around the mountain the people of the little kingdom swarmed down. They had hidden behind rocks and bushes to see how a knight without sword and armor would fight the giant. Now they surrounded Pin, lifted him on their shoulders, and cheering and shouting, carried him down the mountain and into the castle, straight to the king and the princess.

The king embraced him and said, "My brave knight, you freed my country and saved the princess from a terrible fate. Accept your reward. Receive the hand of the princess and the right to the throne!"

At that, voices were heard from the crowd, "But he isn't a knight. He isn't even a man of rank. He is just an ordinary tailor. We saw it with our own eyes and heard it with our own ears."

"Oh dear, oh dear, these bothersome clothes will be my undoing," sighed Pin the tailor. "Now they will even think I am an impostor."

But the king only smiled and said to Pin, "Kneel!" He touched the tailor's shoulder with the tip of his sword and solemnly pronounced, "Herewith I dub you Knight of the Golden Buttonhole!"

Then he bade Pin rise and come forward. He joined the hands of Pin and the princess and wished them great happiness.

The people were so surprised they remained speechless. But only for a moment. Then such cheering and shouting went up it could be heard all over the land. "Let us celebrate the wedding right now," said the king. And so it was done.

On that same day a messenger on horseback was sent to the neighboring country to deliver a magnificent garment to the Lord Chamberlain. He arrived just in time for the grand ball.

On the parcel was written:

TO: MY LORD CHAMBERLAIN

FROM: PIN,

    KNIGHT OF THE GOLDEN BUTTONHOLE

    AND FUTURE KING,

    FORMERLY PIN THE TAILOR.